3-09

DATE DUE

	AUG 0 4 2016
APR 0 8 2009	JUL 1 9 2017
MAY 2 9 2009	
JUN 1 5 2009	
AUG 1 7 2009	
AUG 2 0 2009	
DEC 0 7 2009	
3-18-10	
APR 0 6 2010	
June 01-2010	
JUL 2 7 2010	
AUG 1 2 2010	
AUG 2 6 2010	
NOV 1 1 2010	
1-2-15	
1-27-16	
APR 2 7 2016	
JUN 1 5 2016	

BRODART   Cat. No. 23-221

Three Wishes

by Catherine Lukas
illustrated by Susan Hall

Ready-to-Read

SIMON SPOTLIGHT/NICK JR.
New York   London   Toronto   Sydney

Based on the TV series *Nick Jr. The Backyardigans*™ as seen on Nick Jr.®

SIMON SPOTLIGHT
An imprint of Simon & Schuster Children's Publishing Division
1230 Avenue of the Americas, New York, New York 10020
© 2007 Viacom International Inc.
Nick Jr. The Backyardigans, and all related titles, logos, and characters are trademarks
of Viacom International Inc. NELVANA™ Nelvana Limited. CORUS™ Corus Entertainment Inc. All rights reserv
All rights reserved, including the right of reproduction in whole or in part in any form.
SIMON SPOTLIGHT, READY-TO-READ, and colophon are registered trademarks of Simon & Schuster, Inc.
Manufactured in the United States of America
First Edition
2 4 6 8 10 9 7 5 3 1
Library of Congress Cataloging-in-Publication Data
Lukas, Catherine.
Three wishes / by Catherine Lukas ; illustrated by Susan Hall. — 1st ed.
p. cm. — (Ready-to-read)
"Based on the TV series Backyardigans as seen on Nick Jr."
ISBN-13: 978-1-4169-3437-0
ISBN-10: 1-4169-3437-5
I. Hall, Susan, 1940-   . II. Title.
PZ7.L97822Thr 2007
2006020328

Castaways  , ,

TYRONE PABLO

and are stuck

TASHA

on an .

ISLAND

"I am thirsty,"

says  .

TYRONE

"I am bored,"

says .

PABLO

"I am tired

of wearing rags,"

says  .
TASHA

"Look! A  !"
BOTTLE

says  .
TYRONE

 wades in and gets it.
PABLO

dries it off.

TASHA

WHOOSH!

 puffs out

SMOKE

of the !

BOTTLE

"I am Genie  !
UNIQUA
You may have **3** wishes!"
THREE
"A genie? Cool!"

says  .
TYRONE

"I am thirsty,"
says  .
TYRONE

"I wish I had a huge,
cold  of juice!"
GLASS

"Your wish is my command," says Genie . UNIQUA

WHOOSH!

"I wish I had something new to do," says .

PABLO

"Your wish is my command,"

says Genie . UNIQUA

POOF!

"I wish I had something

nice to wear," says  .

TASHA

"Your wish is my command,"

says Genie  .

UNIQUA

ZAP!

"That is **3** wishes,"
<small>THREE</small>
says Genie  .
<small>UNIQUA</small>
"My work here is done!"

"But how will we get off
this  ?" asks  .
ISLAND   TASHA

"We are doomed!"

says .
PABLO

Wait! I have an idea!"

says  .

TYRONE

"Maybe we can put
our wishes together."

"The  can be a boat.
SURFBOARD

The  can be a mast,
STRAW

and the , a sail."
DRESS

"Cool! You made a  !"
SAILBOAT

says Genie .
UNIQUA

"But sailing home
will take too long.
I am hungry!"
ZAP!

"Time for a snack!"

says .
UNIQUA

"And a cold  of juice!"
GLASS

says .
TYRONE